The East Pudding Chronicles

TALE OF THE TWINKLES

WRITTEN BY

CHRISTOPHER BERRY

ILLUSTRATED BY EMILY HARPER

Printed in the UK by Lulu.com

ISBN 978-1-291-60382-8

For Dad
Because one of my favourite traditions
is walking the dogs after Christmas lunch
when the roads are empty

THE EAST PUDDING CHRONICLES
Tale of the Twinkles

Chapter One
Granny Tells a Story

It was just gone 2pm on Christmas Day and everyone at Number One, Cherry Street, in the village of Dandiest Pug, was preparing to sit down to eat Christmas lunch. Mum and Dad had brought in a plate of carved turkey, together with warmed bowls of Yorkshire puddings, roast potatoes, pigs in blankets, parsnips, carrots and broccoli and a jug of steaming country gravy.

George and Georgina were sat at the dining table with Granny and Grandad and their Uncle Rusty, who had been making Georgina laugh with his jokes. They were all waiting patiently for the food to arrive. Granny was on her second glass of sherry and feeling cheeky. Mum had decorated the table with Roses and Quality Street chocolates, which were for everyone to pick at after dinner and before pudding. But naughty Granny kept sneaking green triangles, strawberry creams and hazelnut whirls into her mouth while Mum and Dad weren't looking. They were busy toing and froing from the kitchen.

Meanwhile, Dipstick, the family dog, was sat in between Granny's legs, panting and dribbling on her skirt. He could see that Granny was eating chocolates. Of course, seeing other people eating made him want food, too. He also knew that Granny had a secret packet of doggy biscuits in her pocket, so he'd been following her around ever since she arrived. Never one to resist the pleading face of a fluffy little dog, Granny kept sneaking him doggy biscuits under the table.

"Oooo, looks yummy," said George, licking his lips, when all of the food had arrived. "Can we tuck in?"

"Photos first!" said Mum cheerily, and everybody groaned.

The next five to ten minutes were spent taking photographs of the family from every angle in existence. Issues such as "Georgina, put that tongue in!" and "Granny, you're not looking!" and "Rusty, your eyes are weird!" and "George, your eyes are shut!" made it take even longer. The food all went cold in the meantime, meaning that Mum and Dad had to do the toing and froing to the kitchen all over again - in order to warm up the bowls of food in the microwave!

When everyone finally sat down to eat, Mum gasped in shock and said, "Where have all the chocolates gone?!"

Looking innocent, Granny said quickly, "It was Georgina. Naughty girl."

"Granny!" cried Georgina, shocked by Granny's little lie. "It wasn't me! Granny's pants are on fire!"

"Granny... was that a porky?" asked Mum.

"Maybe..." Granny smirked. "You shouldn't tempt an old lady with so many yummy chocolates!"

"Deary me!" said Mum.

"HUNGRY!" shouted George. The sooner they ate, the sooner Dad and Uncle Rusty could take Dipstick out for a walk… and the sooner presents could be opened!

"Wait a minute, George," said Dad. "We've all got to pull our crackers first. You know that!"

Above all their plates, next to their dessert spoons, was a Christmas cracker. Crackers were little cardboard tubes that always contained a little toy, a paper crown and slip of paper with a joke on it. And they were always wrapped in colourful, shiny, foil paper and looked like giant wrapped sweets. Two people would pull each end of the wrapper and the cracker would make a huge POP! as it tore in two. Then the toy, the crown and the joke would fall out. Christmas lunch always involved pulling Christmas crackers just before the meal.

So everyone started pulling their crackers with the person sat next to them. There were lots of POPs and lots of little plastic toys exploding all over the dining table. Spinning tops, jumping frogs, mini water guns, whistles, yoyos, toy cars and marbles went everywhere. Everyone put on their paper crowns (even grumpy Grandad!) and then, one by one, everyone started reading their jokes.

"What do you call a one-legged donkey?" asked George.

"I don't know, George," said Mum. "What do you call a one-legged donkey?"

"A wonkey!"

The whole table groaned. Granny giggled.

"What's furry and minty?" asked Georgina. "A polo bear!"

More groans. Even Dipstick groaned at that one.

"What did Mrs Claus say to Santa when he was about to set off?" asked Dad. "Looks like rain, dear!"

Everyone rolled their eyes.

"How do snowmen get around?" asked Uncle Rusty. "They ride on icicles!"

"Oh, they're terrible!" said Georgina.

"They really are!" Granny agreed. "That's what makes them so good! I've got the funniest one... A man walked into a bar..."

Everyone shouted, "OUCH!"

"Oh, we've all heard that one, have we?" Granny smiled.

"Granny, this one's really funny!" giggled Mum. "Why are chocolate buttons rude? Because they're Smarties in the nude!"

"Mine isn't funny," murmured Grandad with a forlorn face. "Mine is sad. Why couldn't the skeleton go to the Christmas party? He had nobody to go with."

Georgina laughed. "Well it is a bit funny, Grandad!"

"Not really. What's funny about a lonely skeleton?"

"No, Grandad. He's a skeleton. He had no BODY to go with."

"Why should he have no friends just because he's a skeleton?" asked Grandad. "Poor skeleton!"

"Oh, never mind, Grandad!" Georgina huffed irritably.

Now that all the jokes had been read, Dad announced, "Right, George! Now we can tuck in!"

Finally, the family ate their scrumptious dinner (which had gone a little bit cold for a second time because of all the cracker-pulling and joke-telling). Afterwards, Mum and Dad were about to get up and start clearing the table, ready for pudding, when Georgina decided to ask a question. One she had been waiting to ask for a little while.

"Why do we pull crackers at Christmas lunch? What is a Christmas cracker anyway? And why do they have toys and paper crowns and jokes inside them? And why are the jokes so bad?"

"Sounds like it's time for another of Granny's stories," said Dad, grinning.

"Yes! Yes!" George cheered impatiently. "Please tell us!"

"Well, all right then," said Granny, sipping her sherry and finishing off a fudge finger, literally the last chocolate left on the table. Dipstick was asleep at her feet, dreaming about his dinner even though his tummy was full of doggy biscuits.

"This is a tale about the Twinkles," said Granny. "Timothy, Tiberius and Charlie-Basil Twinkle. It takes place at Christmas time in East Pudding, several years before what happened to Mrs Mistle. And it's a story about the first ever Christmas cracker…."

Chapter Two
Murmur's Machine

A long, long time ago in a village called East Pudding, there lived a married couple called Tiberius and Timothy Twinkle, who had a son called Charlie-Basil.

Now Tiberius Twinkle had another name amongst the villagers of East Pudding. They called him the 'Toy King'. This is because he was the village's toymaker. He made all sorts of fun toys for the children of the village (and some of the young-at-heart grown-ups too). These included slinkies, teddy bears, pogo sticks, rubber ducks, building blocks, bouncy balls, skittles and drums. Everyone loved Tiberius' toys so much that they started calling him the Toy King. And Tiberius loved being

called the Toy King so much that he made himself lots of different coloured crowns to wear around the village.

Timothy Twinkle was also very popular amongst the villagers – but for a totally different reason. He was the joker of the village, the person who made everyone laugh. He always told the best and cleverest jokes and was always capable of brightening everyone's day. Not only that, but Timothy was the village candymaker. He loved making sweets, chocolates, cakes and cookies.

The 1st of December every year, the beginning of the Christmas season, was also Sweets and Smiles Day. In the afternoon, Timothy would visit everyone in the village and hand out free baskets of marshmallows, jelly babies, lollies, chocolate buttons, fondant fancies, Battenberg cakes and chocolate chip cookies. Then, in the evening, everyone gathered in the village square and Timothy would tell lots of hilarious jokes. Sweets and Smiles Day always put everyone in the mood for Christmas.

There was, of course, one person who lived nearby in the dark depths of Pudding Woods, in a lonely castle, who was NOT a fan of Sweets and Smiles Day. The evil witch, Murmur. She hated Timothy and Tiberius because they brought so much joy to East Pudding, particularly at Christmas time. So she hatched a plan to get rid of them and put an end to Sweets and Smiles Day for good.

She built a frightening machine in the dungeon of her castle. A machine that could change people's bodies. Turn them half-human, half-something-else. It was dome-shaped and white, a bit like an igloo, and had two, fat, metal tubes coming out of it. These tubes were like enormous hollow tentacles, operated by a remote control. One of the tubes would suck up the person into the machine. The other tube would suck up the something-else.

Murmur tested the machine on her chief servant, Mr Weenie, a tall, thin man who had been by Murmur's side from the beginning. She used her remote control to get one of the tentacle-tubes to suck up Mr Weenie into the machine. The other tube sucked up a wasp that was flying around the dungeon in that moment. The machine turned Mr Weenie half-man and half-wasp. He had become a hideous, black and yellow, winged monster. And because the newly transformed Mr Weenie spat a lot when he spoke, Murmur decided to change his name to Spit.

She called the machine the Ultimate Blender. Once she knew that it worked, on November 30th, the night before Sweets and Smiles Day and the beginning of the Christmas season, she ordered Spit and her vultures to fly to East Pudding and kidnap Tiberius and Timothy and bring them to the castle. She also ordered them to bring a basket of Timothy's sweets, cakes and chocolates, and a chest of Tiberius' toys.

"What are you going to do to us?!" screamed Timothy when he and Tiberius arrived in Murmur's dungeon.

"I'm going to put an end to your reign of joy over East Pudding, Timothy Twinkle!" Murmur shrieked gleefully.

"Why don't we all just calm down and have a nice cup of tea?" said Tiberius in a soothing voice.

"Shut up, Toy King!" snapped Murmur. "You sound just like Mumble! He thinks tea is the answer to everything, too!"

"It normally is, Murmur."

19

"You will NOT address me by name, Toy King! You will address me as Your Majesty!"

"But you're not Queen of anything!" Tiberius reasoned.

"I am Queen of West Pudding!" Murmur argued, her face red, her eyes sparking and her fingers curling with fury.

"Not anymore." Tiberius shook his head sadly.

"Shut up! Spit! Vultures! Move them into position!" Murmur ordered, and Spit buzzed forwards and poked Tiberius in the back. One of the vultures flapped over to Timothy and jabbed him with its arched beak. The two men were forced to walk towards Murmur's huge machine.

"Wait!" cried Timothy in fright. "Let's talk about this! Murmur, you don't have to do this. You, too, could enjoy the things we give to the village. Tiberius could make you a lovely, fluffy teddy bear to give you some comfort in this cold castle of yours. And I'd be happy to give you a basket of jelly beans and liquorice if you'd like! Homemade and delicious! And why don't I tell you a few of my best jokes? I bet you all the gold coins in my pocket I could make you laugh!"

"ENOUGH!" Murmur bellowed, her voice echoing up through the castle, causing one of the turrets to crack slightly. "I don't want anything from you! Except SILENCE!"

She tapped some buttons on her remote control. The huge tentacle-tubes came to life and rose into the air. The vulture moved Timothy forwards, till he was standing on a white, square panel that had been placed on the stone floor. Timothy realized the panel was a special magnet, magnetising not just metal but all types of materials, including the leather that Timothy's shoes were made of. Suddenly he couldn't move his feet.

Meanwhile, Spit grabbed the basket of sweets, chocolates and cakes and flew it across the dungeon to place it on another white, magnetic panel on the floor.

As Murmur kept pushing buttons on her remote, one of the huge, twisting tubes snaked towards Timothy and sucked him up like a giant hoover. The other tube curled towards the basket of sweets and sucked it up too.

Murmur listened to Timothy's screams as he and the basket of sweets were pulled inside the dome-shaped body of the Ultimate Blender and churned together, round and round, as if they were inside a washing machine. The whole thing made a terrible whirring noise.

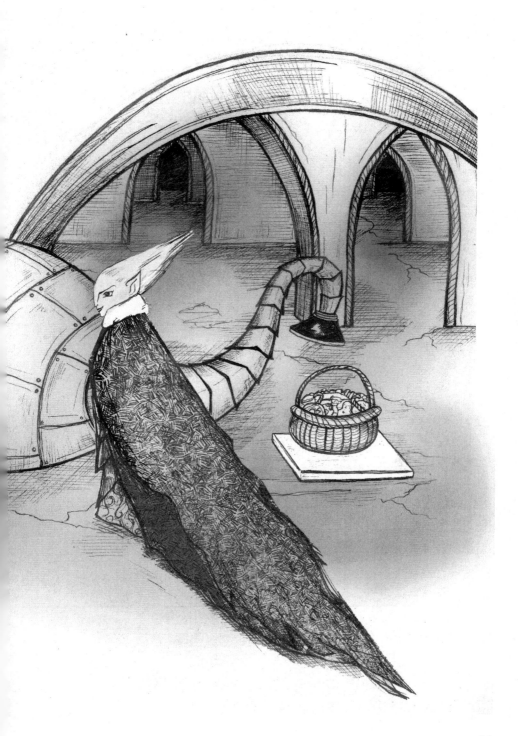

Minutes later, the noise died away and the Ultimate Blender powered down. The tube that had sucked up Timothy sprang to life again and this time, it spat Timothy out onto the floor.

"Oh my!" gasped Tiberius, his mouth wide open in horror. "What has that thing done to you!"

Both of Timothy's arms were now marshmallow flumps. He had chocolate fingers. His middle was a giant ring doughnut with strawberry icing. Half of his brain was made of cake. And one of his legs was made of liquorice allsorts. So now Timothy walked with a limp. But the Ultimate Blender had given Timothy a walking stick made of candy to help him – a red and white candy cane.

Pop!

"What was that?!" asked Tiberius.

"That was me… I, er, I passed wind," whispered Timothy sheepishly.

Indeed, the loud, sharp pop that had just echoed through the dungeon was Timothy breaking wind. It sounded like a balloon exploding.

POP!

"Was that you again?" asked Tiberius.

"Yes…" said Timothy quietly. "I can't help it… there's this strange bubbling in my stomach!"

24

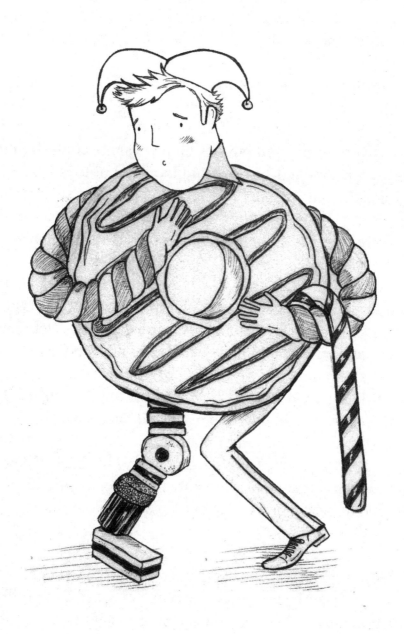

POP! POP!
POP!!

The reason for Timothy's sudden bout of bottom burps was because his stomach was not just a ring doughnut with strawberry icing. The doughnut had a filling. And that filling was popping candy!

Murmur began to laugh hysterically. "Now it's your turn, Toy King!"

As Murmur pressed buttons on her remote control, Spit and the vultures moved Tiberius and the chest of toys into place. The Ultimate Blender powered up again and sucked them inside, churning them together. When the machine spat Tiberius out, Timothy was just as shocked at what it had done to his husband.

Tiberius used to be a rather plump man. Now he was tall and thin, like he'd been stretched. His arms and legs were long, lanky, soft and bendy, as if they were made of rubber. Oh – wait. That's because they *were* made of rubber. Oh my goodness! His neck was a slinky! Which meant that his head was bobbing around all over the place and his crown kept falling off! And finally, if all of that wasn't bad enough, there was a mysterious wooden key sticking out of his back. Tiberius would soon learn that he now operated like clockwork. He would need to be 'wound up' with the key if he ran out of energy.

Murmur burst out laughing once again. "It worked!" she cackled triumphantly. "Now, gentleman, you're free to go! I tell you what, though. I imagine you're going to have some trouble getting back to East Pudding in the state you're both in. So I'll do this one thing for you and have Spit and my vultures fly you back to East Pudding. It's the least I can do!"

Murmur watched Spit and her vultures fly away from the castle with the half-human, half-toy Tiberius and the half-human, half-sweet Timothy. She rippled with evil laughter and didn't stop laughing until the morning. As she did, a light snow began to fall outside.

Chapter Three
The End of Sweets and Smiles Day?

The following morning, Timothy and Tiberius were back in East Pudding. Charlie-Basil came running excitedly into his fathers' bedroom to greet them and wish them a happy Sweets and Smiles Day. Then he saw that Timothy had a great big hole through his stomach and was lifting his liquorice allsorts leg out of bed. And he saw Tiberius' floppy head dangling across the floor on the end of his slinky neck. So Charlie-Basil swiftly fainted.

"Oh dear," said Timothy. "I think we best make him some tea."

Timothy lifted Charlie-Basil into his arms and struggled downstairs, being careful to watch his footing. He made sure to use his candy cane. Tiberius followed, but his long, stretchy legs got tangled and he tripped, rolling down the stairs. His limbs became knotted as he tumbled over and over, his slinky neck opening and closing as it bounced along with him.

He ended up
a big, jumbled ball
of rubber and metal and wood at the bottom of the stairs!

Some time later, after Timothy brewed tea while Tiberius broke free of himself, Charlie-Basil came around to the smell of tea tickling his nostrils. (It had taken Timothy half an hour to make it, as his chocolate fingers kept melting each time he touched the kettle).

"What happened to you both?" Charlie-Basil asked his fathers, waking up on the sofa.

"Murmur happened," Tiberius grumbled grimly. "She used some weird machine to make us like this."

Pop!

Charlie-Basil gasped. It was quite a big pop and it startled him.

"Sorry, that was me," said Timothy. "That happens too. I'm breaking wind nearly every five minutes because my doughnut stomach is full of popping candy."

"What are you going to do?" asked Charlie-Basil.

"Not a lot we can do," said Timothy sadly. "Our lives are pretty much over. It's just taken me half an hour to make you a cup of tea, so I think sweet-making is out of the question. And just look at Dad. He's now a living toy who can't keep his head on straight. I can't see how he's going to be making any more toys."

Charlie-Basil looked at Tiberius. "But Dad, you're the Toy King and it's less than a month till Christmas! All the parents in the village will be coming to you to buy presents for their children!" Then he looked at Timothy. "And Pa, it's Sweets and Smiles Day TODAY!"

"We know, son," said Tiberius. "But I think my…. maaa… maa." Suddenly Tiberius' sentence seemed to fall out of his mouth. His eyes shut and his head dipped, causing his slinky neck to open and stretch and his head to fall off his shoulders onto the floor.

"Dad?" yelped Charlie-Basil with panic in his voice.

"Don't panic!" announced Timothy quickly. "Just need to wind him up!" He rushed over to Tiberius and turned the wooden clockwork key in his back. Tiberius' eyes opened again and he lifted his head back onto his shoulders to finish his sentence.

31

"…maaa… my reign as the Toy King has come to an end," Tiberius finished. "And I think Sweets and Smiles Day is just going to have to be cancelled."

"No!" shouted Charlie-Basil angrily. "This just won't do! I'm not letting that horrible witch spoil everything!"

Charlie-Basil jumped up and lurched out of the front door, dashing across East Pudding to Mumble's castle.

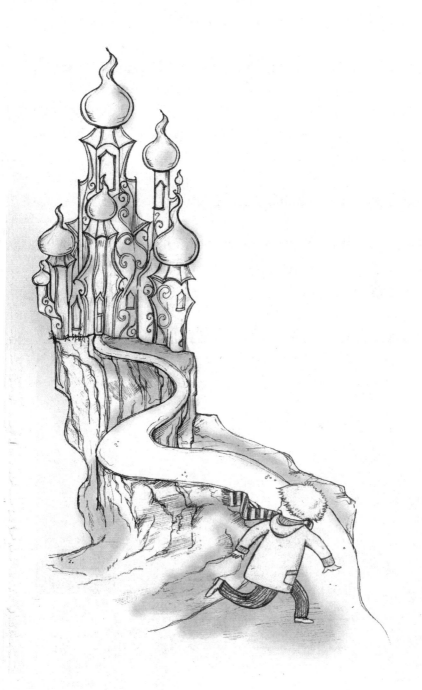

"Mumble, I need your help!" Charlie-Basil yelled as he charged into Mumble's throne room.

"Yes, there's some cheese in the fridge in the kitchens. Help yourself," replied Mumble, completely engrossed in a game of giant chess with Bumfy the comfy chair. He was trying to work out what his next move was and didn't even look up as Charlie-Basil ran in.

"What?" cried Charlie-Basil.

"Next Wednesday," replied Mumble, still staring at the huge chessboard in the middle of the throne room. He was clearly deep in thought.

"I've got you, haven't I!" laughed Bumfy gleefully. "Haha! You're losing to a chair."

"I'm not losing!" Mumble insisted. "I'm just un-doodling my noodle."

"Mumble, I know you're in the middle of something," Charlie-Basil quietly tried to interrupt. "But I really need your help."

"Yes," said Mumble, still staring at the chessboard.

"Mumble? Are you even listening to me?" Charlie-Basil cried crossly.

"Yes. Of course you can borrow my scissors," Mumble replied.

Charlie-Basil marched forwards and tapped Mumble on the arm. Finally the very distracted wizard twirled around with a flurry. "Oh, sorry, young fellow! I didn't see you come in!" he squeaked. "What can I do for you?"

"Murmur's done something horrible to my fathers," said Charlie-Basil. "Pa is saying that Sweets and Smiles Day is cancelled because he can't make sweets anymore. And Dad is saying that his toy-making days are over. They need your help."

"They shall have it, young Sir," replied Mumble. "This game shall have to wait, Bumfy. We have work to do!"

"I'm sure you'd just LOVE to delay this game, since you're loooosing, Bumbly Mumbly!" laughed Bumfy.

"Don't call me that, Lumpy!"

"Hey, I'm not lumpy! I'm comfy Bumfy!"

Mumble chuckled. "Now Charlie-Basil, you head back into the village. I will gather some friends to help and we'll be along in a moment. All right?"

"Yes! Thank you, Mumble!" Charlie-Basil smiled.

Mumble proceeded to call on the services of some of his castle friends, as well as some of the villagers of East Pudding, in order to help the Twinkles get back on their feet. He found both Twinkles sitting in their house, sad and depressed that for the rest of their lives everything was going to be more difficult.

But Mumble was not about to let them feel sorry for themselves!

He ordered them to get up, put on a brave face and start getting used to their new bodies. Mumble, Bumfy, Mrs Bollybongo and the Jelly brothers – Mr Jellybum and Mr Jellylegs – helped Tiberius to carefully balance his wonky head on his slinky neck so that his crown would stay on, and get used to his rubbery limbs. Then they set about helping Tiberius to make some new toys. A slow process, as they had to keep winding Tiberius up when he got tired. But they got there.

Mrs Carter, Mrs Mistle, Mr Bottletopper and Drop the cookie jar all helped Timothy to walk more effectively on his liquorice allsorts leg and use his candy cane, and get used to his chocolate fingers. Because half of Timothy's brain was made of cake, he had trouble remembering the recipes for his sweets, chocolates, cakes and cookies. But Mrs Mistle, who was a keen baker herself and was often inspired by Timothy's cooking, helped him to remember. Drop the cookie jar was, of course, an expert in cookie-making and Mr Bottletopper could make mince pies in his sleep. So they all made an excellent sweet-making team!

Sweets and Smiles Day went ahead as planned. Mumble and Mrs Carter helped Timothy to give out his freshly made sweets, cakes, chocolates and cookies to everyone in East Pudding that afternoon, and later, everyone gathered in the village square to hear Timothy's jokes.

Unfortunately, because Timothy's brain was half-cake, his jokes were not what they used to be.

"What do you call a train loaded with toffee?" Timothy asked the crowd. "A chew chew train!"

There were a few little sniggers in the crowd. Most people just looked at each other, confused.

Timothy continued. "What do hedgehogs have for lunch? Prickled onions!"

Some of the crowd started to laugh nervously. "Ha ha… urm… ha," murmured Mr Dumples, shrugging his shoulders as he looked at his wife.

Timothy didn't let the lack of response from the crowd bother him. He carried on. "What did the fireman's wife get for Christmas? A ladder in her stocking!"

Some of the ladies in the crowd laughed. Most people were still rather confused. The jokes weren't as funny as they were before! They were… bad!

"What did the letter say to the stamp?" said Timothy.

"Stick with me and we'll go places!"

Charlie-Basil burst out laughing. The rest of the crowd was silent to begin with, but when they saw Charlie-Basil rolling on the ground with laughter, some of them started giggling too. The laughing spread, until all the villagers had exploded with wild hilarity!

Timothy smiled. The villagers smiled back at him. The jokes were bad, but they were so bad they were good!

Despite Murmur's attempts to ruin it, Sweets and Smiles Day was a success and the Christmas season had begun. And the Toy King still had his crown. With everyone's help, Tiberius had managed to make dozens of new and exciting toys that all the parents in the village would be able to buy from him as presents for their children in time for Christmas.

Murmur was watching a ripply image of all of this inside

her cauldron of what looked like blood, deep in the depths of her castle.

"That village really will be the death of me!" she screamed, her furious voice bouncing off the cracked, bug-covered walls. "Seriously! That whole village is infected with happiness!"

"But infections have to die, Your Majesty," hissed Spit, hovering above Murmur's shoulder. "Infections have to die so that people can get better."

"You're right, Spit," Murmur snarled. "Those Twinkles haven't heard the last from me. Next year, I promise you. Next year, those Twinkles will DIE!"

Chapter Four
The Twinkles Are Kidnapped Again!

The following year, on the night before Sweets and Smiles Day, Tiberius and Timothy were getting ready. Timothy was in the kitchen cooking peppermint creams, marzipan balls covered in chocolate and lots of tasty sweets out of honeycomb and jelly. At the same time he was practising aloud some of his newly written (but still terrible) jokes. Tiberius was in the living room putting the finishing touches – a spot of paint and varnish here and there – on some of his latest toys. He had decided to invite all the children into his house on Sweets and Smiles morning to play with some of the newest toys, in order to get them excited about Christmas.

But Murmur had other plans. After Timothy and Tiberius had finished their preparations, they put Charlie-Basil to bed and sat out in the garden for a little while, listening to the sounds of the owls and watching the moon-washed sky fill up with a flurry of white, sparkling snowflakes. The first snow of winter.

Suddenly, through the snow, came a flock of hideous birds – vultures – whooshing towards them as if they were diving for their prey. But they were. Timothy and Tiberius were their prey.

The vicious vultures grabbed Timothy and Tiberius before they had a chance to run, clutching them in their huge, arched claws and dragging them into the sky. They carried them from East Pudding back to Murmur's dungeon beneath her castle.

"Oh, great," muttered Tiberius. "Back here again. This is becoming an annual tradition."

"For the sake of all that is sweet and chocolatey, what on earth do you want with us this time, Murmur? Haven't you done enough? Can't you just leave us alone?" cried Timothy breathlessly.

"I've told you before, Candyman! Both of you will address me as YOUR MAJESTY!" Murmur's voice shook the walls.

"Oh, just get on with it," snapped Tiberius. "Whatever you're going to do with us this time, it can't be as bad as last time. So bring it on."

"Oh, you're wrong, Toy King," Murmur cackled. "You're so wrong. Spit! Tie them up!"

Spit buzzed towards them with a thick length of rope. He bound them together with the rope, tying a solid knot around their waists. (Okay, so Timothy didn't really have a waist because his middle was a ring doughnut. So the vultures had to tie the rope through the hole in the doughnut).

"Vultures!" Murmur's horrific black vultures skulked towards her, their claws clicking against the stone floor. "Wrap them up in foil paper, just like we discussed."

"What?" squeaked Timothy, bewildered by Murmur's actions. "What are you doing?"

"I'm getting rid of you for good, Timothy Twinkle," said Murmur. "What do you know of the Giants who live in Pudding Peaks?"

"Not much. They tend to steer clear of East Pudding."

"They do indeed. But I happen to know rather a lot about them. I know that they're taller than this castle. I know that they drool a lot and don't say much. I know that they sleep during the day. And I also know… that they're very fond of eating sweets…"

"Oh my!" yelped Tiberius, suddenly afraid. "What are you going to do to us?"

"Is that not obvious yet?" Murmur laughed. "My vultures here are going to wrap you up in shiny, colourful paper so that you look like a giant wrapped sweet. Then they are going to fly you to Pudding Peaks and leave you on a rock somewhere so that the Giants will come and eat you!"

"No!" screamed Timothy. "You can't! We have a son! Charlie-Basil! You will make him an orphan if you kill us!"

"You should have thought of that, Candyman, before you decided to spread so much joy with your jokes and sweets. My plan to destroy Christmas is never going to work with you and the Toy King around."

"What is wrong with you?" asked Tiberius. "Why do you want to destroy Christmas?"

"Because Christmas is a MISTAKE!" Murmur yelled, her voice making her own vultures cower. "Christmas was never supposed to happen! And I'm going to put an end to it! Christmas has gone too far… and it will go NO FURTHER!"

"This plan is ridiculous!" shouted Tiberius. "It won't work! You say the Giants like eating sweets. Well, as soon as they open the sweet wrapper and find us inside, they won't want to eat us anymore!"

"Are you sure about that, Toy King?" said Murmur with a wicked grin. "Remember – your husband is half-sweet!"

"Well I'm not!"

"True, Toy King. I suppose there's nothing tasty about you. But I'll let you in on another little secret I know about the Giants. They're impulsive eaters. They will eat something because it smells good – before they've even realized what it is! That's exactly what they'll do to you! They'll be drawn by the intense smell of candy coming from Timothy Twinkle. Then they'll rip open the sweet wrapper and gobble you both up without even thinking! So, Toy King, this plan is not ridiculous! This plan is marvellous!"

"Murmur, please don't do this!" Timothy begged.

"What did I say?! YOUR MAJESTY!!!"

The vultures surrounded Tiberius and Timothy, snapping at them with their beaks, yanking them onto the hard floor into the centre of an enormous sheet of foil paper. While Timothy continued screaming, the vultures used their feet to roll the paper around the couple and wrap them up tightly in it. They crumpled up both ends and tied each end with a small strip of green ribbon. The paper was gold and red, sparkling and had lots of pretty patterns all over it. When the vultures were done, it really did look like a giant sweet wrapper. Nobody would have guessed that there were actually two people inside it, not a giant sweet.

"Now, my beautifuls," Murmur said to her vultures. "Take these two to Pudding Peaks and leave them for the Giants to feast on!"

"Please! Your Majesty, please stop this!" Timothy wailed from inside the enormous sweet wrapper, his voice muffled by the thick paper.

"Goodbye, Twinkles!" Murmur crowed as the vultures lifted the giant sweet into the air and flew it out of the dungeon. Murmur grinned as she listened to Timothy's frantic screams fade into the shrill wind that whistled around the towers of her castle. Then she hissed menacingly and under her breath, "Merry Christmas."

44

Chapter Five
Charlie-Basil's Sense of Smell

While Timothy and Tiberius struggled to work out what they were going to do, the vultures flew the giant sweet wrapper they were trapped inside across the skies above Pudding Woods. They were heading for Pudding Peaks, the vast, pointy, snow-topped mountains where the Giants lived.

Meanwhile, Charlie-Basil Twinkle couldn't sleep. Even though his fathers had put him to bed several hours before, Charlie-Basil was too excited about Sweets and Smiles Day and getting ready for Christmas to sleep. He eventually decided he was thirsty and went downstairs to get a glass of water. The house was strangely quiet. He figured that his fathers had gone to bed.

But then he saw that the back door was open. It wasn't like them to go to bed and leave the back door open. "Pa? Dad?" Charlie-Basil called as he approached the door.

Charlie-Basil came out into the lightly snow-covered garden. His fathers weren't there. But there was a chair overturned in the snow and a cup of tea, which Tiberius had been drinking, was spilled next to it.

Charlie-Basil ran back into the house, panicked. "Dad? Pa? Are you here?"

No answer.

"Pa? Dad? Where are you!" Charlie-Basil screamed.

Realising that something must have happened to them, Charlie-Basil quickly dug his feet into his slippers and wrapped himself in a big winter coat. He swept out of the front door into the cold, snowy night.

"Dad? Pa?" he called as he wandered through East Pudding. Mrs Carter and Mr Ribbet were woken by Charlie-Basil's cries for his fathers and immediately got dressed so that they could go and help him.

Charlie-Basil wandered to the edge of East Pudding, near to the border of Pudding Woods. He swallowed hard. "Oh… please don't be in there…"

Just before Charlie-Basil stepped into the murky darkness of the trees, he heard the whoosh of giant wings above him. He looked up and saw two black vultures flying a brightly coloured, giant wrapped sweet across the sky.

He might not have thought anything of it had it not been for the smell.

The smell wafted on the snowy wind and invaded his nostrils. Charlie-Basil had a sharp sense of smell and knew immediately what the smell was. He would have recognised it anywhere.

His father, Timothy Twinkle. The thick aroma of chocolate, liquorice and popping candy farts tickled Charlie-Basil's nose.

"Oh my! They've got Pa!" Charlie-Basil realized with horror. "They've probably got Dad too!"

Suddenly Mrs Carter and Mr Ribbet came running up behind Charlie-Basil. "Young Master Twinkle," said Mr Ribbet in a posh voice, his scarf flapping and his glasses threatening to tumble off his nose. "Are you all right?"

"No!" cried Charlie-Basil. "Murmur's got my fathers! She's kidnapped them again!"

"How do you know, dear?" asked Mrs Carter in a soft voice.

"I've just seen her vultures flying what looked like a giant wrapped sweet across the skies above Pudding Woods. I didn't think much of it till the smell hit me! The smell of candy! It was Pa's smell! I know his smell anywhere!"

"Did you see in which direction the vultures were flying this giant sweet?" asked Mr Ribbet.

"North, I think," said Charlie-Basil.

Mrs Carter and Mr Ribbet looked at each other, their eyes full of dread. "Oh no," whispered Mrs Carter. "That means… but that means…!"

Mr Ribbet finished Mrs Carter's sentence for her. "The Giants."

"Giants?" said Charlie-Basil in a high voice. "Dad and Pa told me about the Giants. They told me some people don't even believe in them – because no one's seen a Giant in years!"

"Trust me, little one," said Mrs Carter sadly. "The Giants are real. I can hear them sometimes. Snoring. The pig-like sounds they make carry on the wind."

"Well we need to go quickly and rescue my fathers before the Giants get them!" shouted Charlie-Basil.

"We will require extra assistance, Master Twinkle, if we're going to do that," said Mr Ribbet.

"Agreed," said Mrs Carter. "Let's go and wake Mumble."

Chapter Six
The Giants

Charlie-Basil, Mr Ribbet and Mrs Carter marched across East Pudding to Mumble's castle and asked Chirrup the alarm clock to wake Mumble up. Chirrup remembered that Mumble was usually extra-confused if he was woken up in the middle of the night. So he took a cup of coffee – and nabbed a cookie out of Drop's jar while he was sleeping – and took them up to Mumble for a very early breakfast.

"Rise and shine, Mr Mumble!" chirped Chirrup in a high-pitched, squeaky voice. "You've got work to do!"

"No! No!" Mumble woke with a start and sat up in his huge, four-poster bed suddenly. "You mustn't talk about parsnips like that! They do not have thick skins!"

"Urrrm….. yes," Chirrup said flatly. "Now drink this coffee and eat this cookie so you can wake up properly. The Twinkles need your help!"

Mumble rolled his eyes. "Twinkle, twinkle little onion. How I wonder 'bout your bunion."

"Sir, you're delirious! Snap out of it!"

"Rumble Mumble. Stumble crumble. Jumble." Mumble's voice became quieter as his words faded from his lips and his heavy eyes started to close again. He was falling back to sleep. In a moment he had flopped back onto his pillow.

"EEEEEEE!!!" Chirrup let out the shrillest squeal ever, waking nearly every creature in the castle.

Mumble bolted upright, eyes wide open. "Blimey, Chirrup. Must you shout?"

"Come with me now, Sir! The Twinkles have been kidnapped by Murmur! We think she's trying to feed them to the Giants!" squawked Chirrup.

"Oh my! Then we must go right away!" Mumble launched himself out of bed and did the quickest change out of

his pyjamas that he'd ever done. He hurtled downstairs to the bottom of the castle, where Charlie-Basil, Mr Ribbet and Mrs Carter were waiting.

"Right, Charlie-Basil! Tell me everything!" he boomed as they all swept out of the castle together.

Charlie-Basil told Mumble what had happened as they all embarked on a journey to Pudding Peaks. They arrived shortly after the vultures had left and were flying back to Murmur's castle. They entered a slim, uneven valley of tall boulders and jagged rocks that carved its way through the vast mountains.

"Where are they?!" Charlie-Basil yelled frantically, his eyes searching every rock for any sign of a shiny, red and gold wrapped sweet. "I can't see them!"

"There!" cried Mumble, noticing the glint of gold behind a huge boulder and pointing.

The four of them dashed over to where Mumble was pointing and found the huge, bulging wrapped sweet wriggling and squirming on top of a large, flat rock.

"Dad? Pa? Are you in there?" cried Charlie-Basil.

"Charlie-Basil? Is that you?" Timothy yelped in a muffled voice from inside the wrapper. "Yes, it's me!"

"Quick! Get us out of here!" shouted Tiberius. "The Giants will be here any moment!"

Suddenly, a gigantic thump, as heavy as a house, echoed throughout Pudding Peaks and shook the ground beneath all of them.

"Oh no!" screamed Mrs Carter. "What was that?!"

Another massive thump, this one louder and closer. All around, rocks shuddered and little pebbles jumped. All of their hearts were pounding, even Mumble's.

A Giant's footsteps.

"Quickly!" shrieked Timothy. "Get us out of here!"

Immediately Charlie-Basil tried to undo the knots in the ribbon around each end of the sweet wrapper. But even though his fingers were smaller than everybody else's, the vultures had tied the knots so tight that he couldn't pick them.

"Right, let's just pull this thing apart!" suggested Mumble, lurching forwards and grabbing one end of the giant sweet wrapper. Mrs Carter went and stood by him to help him pull. Charlie-Basil and Mr Ribbet dashed over to the other end. All four of them scrunched a section of the paper in their hands, closed their fingers in firm grips and bent their knees to get ready to pull the sweet wrapper apart.

"Okay. Now PULL!" Mumble instructed.

But as hard as they all tried, they could not rip apart the sweet wrapper. The paper Murmur had used was too strong. She had used paper that only Giants could rip, to make sure that Timothy and Tiberius would not escape.

When Mumble, Mrs Carter and Mr Ribbet all realized that they were not going to be able to rip the paper, they let go. Charlie-Basil carried on pulling. "What are you doing?" he shouted at the others. "The Giants are coming! We need to get this thing open!"

"Charlie-Basil, we have to go," said Mumble sadly. "There's nothing we can do. The paper's too strong. She made it so only Giants can rip it."

"No, we can't give up! You're a wizard! Can't you use a spell to get them out?"

"I'm afraid I don't know any for this, little Twinkle." Mumble dipped his head sadly. "I could turn the whole sweet into a potato. But then your fathers would be a potato. That doesn't really help."

Another massive thud made the rocks quake and the ground shudder beneath their feet.

"Oh my! They're here!" bawled Mrs Carter, pointing a shaky finger towards the two enormous figures that were clod-hopping through the mountains towards them.

"Crumbly crumbs!" Mr Ribbet cried. "There's two of them!"

"Charlie-Basil, go!" Tiberius ordered from inside the sweet. "We don't want you dying with us! Get out of here now!"

"But I have to save you!" Charlie-Basil screamed, tears pouring from his eyes.

"You can't save us, son! But you MUST save yourself! Just know that we will always love you!"

"Charlie-Basil, we've got to go!" shouted Mumble. "I'm sorry!" Mumble grabbed Charlie-Basil's arm and pulled him away from his fathers. Charlie-Basil cried hopelessly as he, Mumble, Mrs Carter and Mr Ribbet leapt over several rocks and boulders. Having run to a safe distance, away from the valley, they hid behind a wide oak tree that was the last bit of green before the chalky mountains.

Charlie-Basil sat with his back against the tree and his head in his hands, crying. Mumble, Mrs Carter and Mr Ribbet watched the two lumbering Giants approach Timothy and Tiberius – all three of them hoping for a miracle.

The Giants were hefty, beefy things with arms the size of trees, big, scraggly beards that were like small forests and gaping eyes. They certainly did drool a LOT, and because they were so huge, their drool was like small waterfalls.

Guided by their noses, the curious Giants plodded heavily towards the pungent smell of chocolate and candy.

One of them, whose name was Fo, eventually caught sight of the bright, sparkly sweet set down on a rock in the valley, and started marching towards it.

The other Giant, Fum, noticed that Fo had spotted something and followed him. Fo picked up the huge sweet and smelled it, his big, fat nose twitching. He was about to rip the sweet wrapper apart to get to what was inside, when Fum rushed over and grabbed one end of the wrapper.

Fo grunted as Fum tried to pull the sweet out of his hand. Fo kept a firm grip on the other end of the wrapper. He pulled on it too.

Meanwhile Timothy and Tiberius, rolling around inside, could tell that the paper was about to rip – at which point they would be gobbled up by one or both of the Giants. Their hearts were pounding and sweat trickled off their foreheads like leaky taps. (Well, in Timothy's case, it wasn't actually sweat. It was sticky sugar syrup).

"Oh my gosh!" whispered Tiberius. "I have an idea!"

"What?" replied Timothy. "What is it?"

"You know what Giants are scared of, don't you?" Tiberius said.

"No. What? Quickly! Tell me! WHAT?!" Timothy squealed.

"Pooooaaa… aaaa."

Tiberius' sentence whistled away at just the wrong moment!

"Oh, for the love of jelly beans!!" Timothy squirmed within the rope that was tied through his ring doughnut middle, struggling to reach Tiberius' clockwork key and turn it. "Wake up! Come oooonnn!"

"oooo… ops and bangs!" Tiberius continued once Timothy had wound him up again. Timothy gasped with relief.

"They hate any loud noises," Tiberius said, "but particularly pops and bangs! That's why they never come to East Pudding – because of Mrs Carter's firework displays!"

"What are you suggesting?" Timothy asked.

"Timothy, I know half your brain is made of cake, but isn't it obvious? You!"

Timothy was confused. "Me?"

"Fart, Timothy! Let out a big fart and it'll scare them off!"

"Tiberius, my bottom burps do make popping sounds. But they'll never be loud enough to scare off a pair of Giants!"

Tiberius reached into a pocket inside his coat and pulled out a can of lemonade. "Try this! If you drink this, it should react with the popping candy in your stomach and make you produce the biggest fart ever!"

Fo and Fum were still pulling on the sweet wrapper, grunting and growling at each other. Mumble, Mrs Carter, Mr Ribbet and Charlie-Basil could not understand what the two

Giants were saying to each other, but in Giant language it was basically – "MINE!" and "NO! MINE! I SAW IT FIRST! YOU MISERABLE LUMP OF POOP!"

"Quickly! Drink it!" Tiberius cried as Timothy poured the lemonade down his throat. "Once the Giants open this thing, we're done for!"

Timothy finished the can and felt his stomach start to bubble violently.

"Oh my!" he yelped. "It's coming!"

Tiberius put his hands over his ears as Timothy let out the biggest fart ever, making an enormous, earth-shattering POP! echo through the mountains of Pudding Peaks.

Right at that same moment, Fo and Fum managed to pull apart the giant sweet wrapper, both stumbling back, while Timothy and Tiberius tumbled out and plunged to the pebbly ground, landing at the Giants' feet.

But Fo and Fum gasped in horror and started trembling, their eyes wide and worried. The huge bang from Timothy's passing wind was still echoing through Pudding Peaks. The Giants hated noises like that. It really frightened them. They threw their hands over their ears as the echo from the bang continued.

A moment later, Fo and Fum backed away, scared that there might be another pop or bang. Both of them dropped the ripped bits of sweet wrapper, turned and started stomping away quickly, disappearing into the shadows of the mountains.

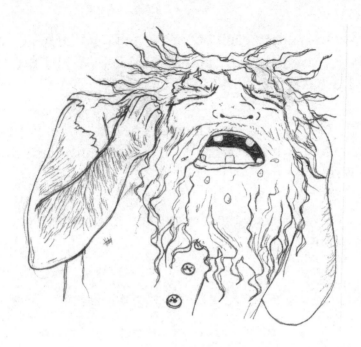

"Dad! Pa!" screamed Charlie-Basil as he ran from the tree that he, Mumble and the others were hidden behind. He rushed over to his fathers, who were struggling to get to their feet, and helped them up. "I really thought I'd lost you there!" He cuddled both of them at once.

Mumble, Mr Ribbet and Mrs Carter walked over to the reunited family, all with big smiles on their faces.

"Timothy, I take it that was you who let out that enormous fart that nearly deafened us all?" said Mumble with a smirk.

"Yup!" said Timothy proudly. "But only because my wonderful husband here remembered that Giants hate loud pops and bangs!" He leaned towards Tiberius and kissed him on the nose.

"I'm so glad you're both okay," said Charlie-Basil, still with tears in his eyes. "I don't know what I would've done if those Giants had eaten you."

"Funny thing is," Timothy said, "I never would've been able to scare the Giants off by letting out a big popping candy fart – had Murmur not made me half-sweet!"

"Indeed!" exclaimed Tiberius. "That horrible witch's plan really did backfire this time!"

"Come on. Let's get you home," said Mumble, placing his hand on Timothy's shoulder. "It's Sweets and Smiles Day tomorrow. Murmur wanted to ruin it. But she failed. And we're going to have the best Sweets and Smiles Day ever."

So Mumble, Mrs Carter, Mr Ribbet and the Twinkles all went back to East Pudding to get a few hours' sleep before the big day.

The following morning, Timothy awoke and, with Charlie-Basil's help, he set about writing some new jokes. Then, with help from Charlie-Basil, Mrs Carter and Mrs Mistle, Timothy made a selection of delicious sweets, chocolates and cakes. He took little baskets of goodies round to everyone in the village that afternoon, so that everyone knew that the Christmas season had arrived.

Because it was Sweets and Smiles Day, Tiberius thought it was a good time to invent a new toy. He wanted to make a toy that would remind everyone of what had happened to him and Timothy. While it was scary for them at the time, he wanted to turn what happened to them into something fun.

So he built an oversized sweet. Basically it was a toilet roll tube wrapped in colourful foil paper and tied at each end so that it looked like a giant wrapped sweet. Inside the tube he put a miniature toy and a paper crown to represent himself. He put in a little slip of paper with a terrible joke on it to represent Timothy. And he made it so two people had to pull the sweet apart to get inside it, just like the Giants did.

But what he also did was put in a 'banger' – a little strip of card that would make a loud bang when the sweet was pulled apart – to represent Timothy's popping candy fart. The fart that frightened away the Giants just as they managed to rip the sweet in two.

He called his new toy a 'cracker' because of the noise it made. People started buying crackers from Tiberius and pulling them all through the Christmas season. But it was Mr and Mrs Dumples who decided that crackers would be a good way of making Christmas dinner more fun. They suggested that people pull crackers before eating, so they can play with the little toys, tell jokes to each other and wear paper crowns and pretend to be the Toy King during dinner. Roast Turkey suddenly became much more interesting.

Tiberius' cracker was a marvellous success. It made sure that nobody ever forgot what had happened to the Twinkles that Christmas, and that Murmur, in trying to spoil Christmas for the people of East Pudding, had been beaten once again.

Chapter Seven
Murmur Goes Mad!

Of course, Murmur saw Timothy and Tiberius escape the Giants. She was down in her dungeon watching the events unfold in a reflection in the bubbling, blood-coloured gunge in her cauldron.

Her rage was bubbling too, and it boiled over when she saw Fo and Fum stomp away in fear. She lost her temper. It did happen occasionally. And it was always a disaster when it did.

"Those fat, stupid imbeciles!" Murmur yelled, her booming voice shaking cobwebs off the walls. "How can they be frightened away so easily?! The wimps! The flabby, slimy, bird-poo-for-brains COWARDS!"

"We can still stop the Twinkles, Your Majesty," said Spit, trying to comfort her. "They cannot survive us a third time."

"Those Twinkles have foiled me at every turn, Spit! WHY?! HOW?!" Murmur's face was red with fury. She picked up her cauldron and hurled it across the room. It cracked apart and thick, hot goo spilled out of it. The goo splashed against the stone floor and hissed as it gave off wisps of steam. One of her vultures was stood nearby and the puddle touched its foot, causing the vulture to melt!

"Your Majesty, perhaps you should calm down," said Spit gently.

"Don't tell me to calm down! Or I'll do to you what I did

to the Fairies!"

"I only mean – "

"SHUT UP, Spit!" Murmur spun in an angry frenzy. Her arms were thrashing and her cloak rose and fell like the waves of Yule Sea. "WHY? Why do I never get my way? Why can't things ever go to plan? WHY?"

"But Your Majesty, watch out!" cried Spit. "You're about to –!"

Suddenly, the Ultimate Blender powered up. The two tentacle-like tubes awoke and started twisting through the air like snakes.

As it was already too late, Spit muttered under his breath the thing he had tried to say – "You're about to… tread on the remote."

In her rage, Murmur had not been watching where she was walking. She had accidentally trodden on the remote control which she used to control the Ultimate Blender.

"What?" Murmur turned round when she heard the mechanical whir of the machine powering up. "NOOOO!!!"

One of the tentacle-tubes lunged at her and sucked her up, whisking her inside the machine. The other tentacle-tube was flailing about, looking for something else to suck up. Finally it twisted towards the back wall of the dungeon, which was crawling in bugs and insects. As it scraped the wall, there was a tiny scorpion scuttling across the brickwork, scrambling for a crack to hide in. But the scorpion never made it and the tube sucked it up, pulling it inside the machine with Murmur.

Spit listened to Murmur's hideous, blood-curdling shrieks as the Ultimate Blender churned her up with the scorpion and then, minutes later, spat her out onto the floor of the dungeon.

Spit gasped as Murmur rose to her feet. As she rose to her *eight* feet. Now she had eight, sharp, pointy scorpion legs. One of her arms was a scorpion pincer. And a massive scorpion tail with a vicious, red stinger curled and swayed behind her. The Ultimate Blender had made her half-witch, half-scorpion.

"Your Majesty! I – I –!" Spit screamed, speechless with shock.

Murmur started to approach him, her ugly scorpion legs clicking against the floor. Her face was twisted with fury. Spit backed away, trembling in fear.

"You – you – what?" said Murmur. "You left the remote control in the middle of the floor for me to step on? Is that what you're trying to say?"

"Your Majesty! It was an accident! I'm sorry!" Spit cried frantically.

"I'm sure you are, Spit," replied Murmur calmly. "I'm sure you are."

This time Spit wasn't looking where he was walking. As he backed away from Murmur, he stepped into the puddle of red goo from Murmur's cauldron. In a moment, the red goo melted Spit and, with a fizzle and a hiss, the half-man, half-wasp was gone.

The vultures fled in horror. They were too frightened to continue being Murmur's servants. Not now that she was a half-scorpion monster. One by one, they flew out of the dungeon, away from the castle and far across the land, never to return.

"That's that, then," said Murmur. "I'm going to need some new servants. I know just the folk. And I'm sure they'll make much better servants than Spit and those useless vultures."

Murmur swept out of the dungeon and down some more steps into a second dungeon that was even deeper underground. For several years, Murmur had kept a large group of people locked up in cages in her second dungeon. Finally they were going to be of some use to her.

She used her scorpion tail to sting them all, filling their veins with her evil. Being half-scorpion could be useful, she discovered. All of the men and women she stung started changing. Their bodies started twisting. Their arms became long and spidery and their ears and noses grew, becoming sharp and pointy. They all became hideous goblins and Murmur came to refer to them all as her 'elves'.

A few weeks later, on Christmas Day, Murmur was sat on her throne. She had ear plugs in her ears so she could block out the sound of Christmas carols carrying on the wind from East Pudding. One of her elves slinked towards her and bowed.

"What is your bidding, Mistress?" asked the elf.

"Build me some better ear plugs," hissed Murmur in reply. "I can still hear the sound of Christmas carols."

"As you wish, Mistress," said the elf obediently.

"What is your name, elf?" asked Murmur.

"I cannot recall my original name, Mistress, but you gave me a new one. Atnas Sualc."

"Yes, of course. Thank you, Atnas. Now get to work."

As Atnas scuttled away, Murmur remembered who he was. She remembered his name before she stung him with her tail and turned him into an evil elf. He was Arthur Nicholas – a name that would forever be lost – just like the village where Arthur Nicholas came from.

West Pudding.

Chapter Eight
Time for Pudding

"What?!" cried Georgina. "West Pudding? What's West Pudding?"

"Ah, that's a story for another day," replied Granny, grinning.

"But Granny, you can't leave it there!" George insisted. "Who were all those people Murmur had in her dungeon? The ones she turned into elves?"

"Like I say, George – a story for another day."

"Oh, GRANNY!" said both George and Georgina together.

"Sorry, children!" said Granny. "But if I tell another story, we'll be here all night! Look. Your Grandad's about to fall asleep in his gravy. And we have presents to open this evening, remember!"

"Oh, all right then!" cried George with wide eyes. "You've persuaded me!"

"And me!" Georgina agreed.

"First thing's first, though!" Dad said, rubbing his hands together proudly. "It's time for pudding! Christmas Pudding with brandy sauce, anyone?"

"Just a tiny sliver for me, please," said Mum. "I really

need to get back on the diet."

"Oh, Mother!" shouted Georgina. "Stop worrying about what you look like! You look very pretty. I'm going to steal all your mirrors."

"And just a smidgen of brandy sauce for me, dear," said Granny. "You make it rather strong and I don't want to end up... under the table!"

Dad got up from the table to take out the dinner plates to the kitchen and dish up the Christmas Pudding and brandy sauce. As he did so, his elbow knocked a branch of the Christmas tree and a candy cane fell off. George was about to get up and hang it back on the branch but Dipstick, now awake again, whooshed across the floor with the speed of a train and gobbled it up.

"So that's why we have candy canes at Christmas, too," realized George. "Because of Timothy Twinkle, the candyman, who had to walk with a candy cane after what Murmur did to him."

73

"I like that story," said Georgina, smiling, touching the paper crown on her head to make sure it was still on straight. "I like stories with happy endings."

"Oh, look!" cried George suddenly. He pointed towards the middle of the table, near to the bowl that had one small sprig of cold broccoli left in it. "There's still a Christmas cracker left!"

One Christmas cracker had been overlooked. George grabbed one end of it and turned around to his sister, who grabbed the other end. "One, two, three!" said George, and the two of them pulled together. With a large POP! the cracker split apart and a miniature slinky, a blue paper crown and a joke sprang out of it, scattering over the table. Georgina reached for the slinky and started playing with it. George reached for the joke to read it out.

"Awww! Looks like Timothy Twinkle wrote this one especially for Tiberius!" George exclaimed.

"What is it?" asked Georgina.

"What did the clock say to the man who was teasing it?" said George.

"I don't know," replied Mum. "What did the clock say to the man who was teasing it?"

"Stop winding me up!"

Dipstick was still crunching on his candy cane. Mum and Georgina chuckled. Uncle Rusty smirked. Granny broke into a fit of giggles. Grandad was asleep in his gravy. A moment later, Dad returned to the table with Christmas Pudding, brandy sauce and a big smile on his face. "Pudding's up!"

ABOUT THE AUTHOR

Of all the books so far, Christopher Berry was the most excited to see Emily Harper's illustrations for *Tale of the Twinkles*, the third book in *The East Pudding Chronicles*. There's a whole load of brand new and bizarre characters introduced in this one, and Christopher is thrilled with the amazing work that Emily has done bringing these characters to life. Spit is terrifying! A few more of George and Georgina's family are introduced too - again based on Christopher's family! Christopher's own Granny was famous for pinching chocolates off the dining table and blaming Christopher's sister, Katie, and Christopher's family having to microwave their dinners because his Mum spends so long taking photographs really does happen!

This year has been eventful for Christopher. He has changed jobs and moved house, but is still writing and busier than ever. He has just moved in with his friend Fabs and knows they're going to have great fun! And Christopher's friend Kerrie had her baby. He is called James. He's full of smiles and already walking!

Visit Christopher's website at www.berrytimebooks.com and you will be able to buy the first two books in the series, *The Christmas Monster* and *The Merry Mrs Mistle*. He looks forward to working with Emily on the next book, which will be all about where Christmas trees came from!

Finally Christopher thought - as this is a book about cracker jokes - that he would share with his readers his favourite joke when he was growing up.

Where would you find a stupid shoplifter?
Squashed under Tescos!

ABOUT THE ILLUSTRATOR

Devastated when she didn't receive her Hogwarts letter, Emily decided to do something just as magical so decided to illustrate and write children's books instead! She has worked on a number of other children's books, both writing her own stories and illustrating for other authors. More of her work can be seen at www.emilyharperillustration.com.

As well as her illustration work, Emily spent last year teaching in a primary school, a great experience as she got to learn all about what kind of books children enjoy. Emily would like to dedicate the illustrations in this book to the fantastic class of children she taught last year as they definitely helped her to keep her imagination alive. This is for you, 3H - keep up those high hopes!

Christopher has created some truly original characters in this book, and Emily has particularly enjoyed drawing the Twinkles. It's not every day you get to draw someone who is part-human, part doughnut! She anticipates even more weird and wonderful characters in the next book, so be sure to visit Christopher's website next Halloween to find out more...